Harry on the Rocks

Susan Meddaugh

Houghton Mifflin Company Boston 2003

Walter Lorraine Books

For Sam and Win

Walter Lorraine (wr) Books

Copyright © 2003 by Susan Meddaugh

All rights reserved. For information about permission
to reproduce selections from this book, write to Permissions,
Houghton Mifflin Company, 215 Park Avenue South,
New York, New York 10003.

www.houghtonmifflinbooks.com

Library of Congress Cataloging-in-Publication Data

Meddaugh, Susan.
  Harry on the rocks / by Susan Meddaugh.
    p. cm.
  Summary: Harry and his boat become stranded on an island,
where he discovers an egg which hatches into a strange lizard
with wings.
  ISBN 0-618-27603-3
  [1. Shipwrecks—Fiction. 2. Islands—Fiction. 3. Eggs—Fiction.
4. Dragons—Fiction.]   I. Title.
PZ7.M51273Har 2003
[E]—dc21

2002009740

Printed in United States of America
WOZ 10 9 8 7 6 5 4 3 2 1

It was a calm day when Harry floated out to sea. He had been rowing peacefully down the river when a seagull mistook his head for a rock. Hoping to break open a tasty clam, the nearsighted bird dropped it on Harry's head. And Harry dropped his oars. The tide, which was going out, took Harry and his little yellow boat along with it.

3

Soon the wind began to blow, and the clear blue sky filled
with clouds. The rain fell, and Harry could no longer see land.
He was scared.

The waves tossed Harry's boat up and down. Harry hung on for his life.

When the storm had finally blown itself out, one last wave
picked up Harry's boat, with Harry in it, and dropped it down
onto solid ground. By then it was late and dark, and Harry was
exhausted. He crawled under the wreck of his boat and fell asleep.

The sea was calm and the sky was blue when Harry woke up the next day. He looked around, and all he saw was sand and rocks.

He walked and walked, and all he found was more rocks and one windblown tree.

Harry sat down in the shade of the tree.

"Rocks," he said. "Nothing but sand and rocks."

Then he noticed one rock that wasn't like all the other rocks.

An egg, thought Harry. *What luck!*

Harry was very hungry. But he didn't think he would like to eat a raw egg.

Perhaps if I leave it in the hot sun, by dinnertime I will have a hard-boiled egg, he thought.

Harry moved the egg to a rock in the sun.

The egg did not cook in the sun. It hatched.
A small but colorful lizard emerged.
Harry stared at the little creature.
No egg for dinner, he thought.

Instead he picked a leaf from the windblown tree. It was plump and juicy, and Harry took a great big bite.
"Ugh," he said. "This tastes exactly like broccoli boiled in skunk cabbage oil!"
But there was nothing else to eat, so he picked a few more leaves and shared them with the little lizard.
"Mmmm," said the lizard.

The next day Harry picked more leaves from the tree
for himself and for the lizard. He saw that the lizard
had grown a lot in one day. He also noticed little wings.
"What on earth are you?" asked Harry. "You look like a lizard,
but you have wings like a bird. Perhaps I have discovered a
missing link," he said. "I think you are a *bizzard*!"

"You ha**v**e wings," he said. "Why don't you fly out
and cat**ch** us a fish."
The biz**z**ard gave him a puzzled look.
"Don't **t**ell me you don't know how to fly," said Harry.
The biz**z**ard hung his head.
"Then **it** is time for you to learn," Harry told him.

The first lesson was flapping.
Just flapping.

The biz**z**ard flapped.

Harry could not stop thinking about food. All around him
sea birds were dipping into the water and coming up with dinner.
"I will go fishing too," said Harry.
But after spending the entire day in the water, Harry had not
caught a single fish.
If only I had wings and a beak, thought Harry.
Then he remembered the bizzard.

The next lesson was flapping
and jumping into the air.
The bizzard flapped, jumped,

and fell.

"Keep trying!" said Harry.

The bizzard flapped, jumped, and fell again. Day after day he flapped and fell and flapped and fell.

But Harry said, "Your wings are getting bigger and stronger. Soon we will have fish for dinner."

"Mmmmm," said the bizzard. He flapped and fell again.

Then, at last, the bizzard flapped and did not fall.

He flew.
He swooped out over the water.
The birds stayed far away from him.
"Good boy!" shouted Harry when
the bizzard dropped a fat fish on the
rock in front of him.
"Now, if only we had a fire," he said,
"we could have a fish banquet!"

"Mmmmmmm!" said the bizzard.
He smiled. A big, toothy smile.
"You are not a bizzard," said Harry, and suddenly he was very
frightened. "You are a DRAGON!"

Harry dived under his broken boat. He stayed there all day and all night. Every so often he would yell: "Go away!" or "There's nobody in here!"

When he finally poked his head out, the dragon was gone. *That was a close call,* thought Harry. *To think that I actually fed a dragon and taught him how to fly! I'm lucky I discovered what he really was before he got tired of leaves.*

Harry spent the rest of the day trying to catch fish. But he had leaves again for dinner.

The next few days were much the same. The leaves were almost gone from the tree and, what was worse, Harry was lonely.

Except for the fact that he was probably going to eat me, that dragon was good company, he thought.

Harry spent long hours on the beach. He hoped to see a boat on the horizon. But he never did.

Two weeks after the dragon had disappeared, Harry woke
up to a dark sky. Once again the wind began to blow, the
rain fell, and the waves crashed on the shore. Each wave
seemed bigger than the last as Harry hopped from rock to
rock, looking for higher ground.

In desperation he climbed to the top of the windblown tree.
But this was one storm the old tree would not survive. There
was a terrible roar as the biggest wave of all hit the trunk of
the tree, ripping roots from the rocks that held them.

In the two weeks that had passed, the dragon had
grown even larger. He flew high above the clouds,
and Harry held on tight. When they had flown
beyond the storm, Harry looked down and saw
land. Not sand and rocks, but grass and
trees and houses.

He even saw his own little white house with red shutters. "Down please," said Harry, and they made a perfect, soft landing in Harry's backyard.

"You saved my life," said Harry. He couldn't help wondering
why the dragon had come back.
The dragon smiled.
"Mmmm," he said. "Mmmmm . . . Mmmmmm . . . MOM!"